Ridge Danyers - Marple Site

M0031906

For Morgan – M.P.

For Marc – M.F.

First published in Great Britain in 1998 by
Macdonald Young Books
an imprint of Wayland Publishers Ltd
61 Western Road
Hove
East Sussex
BN3 1JD

Find Macdonald Young Books on the internet at http://www.myb.co.uk

First published by Zirkoon Publishers, Amsterdam 1998
Concept and illustrations copyright © Mylo Freeman 1998
Text copyright © Maartje Padt 1998

Printed and bound in Singapore
British Library Cataloguing in Publication Data available.

ISBN: 0 7500 2592 1

SHANTI
the zebra

Maartje Padt • Mylo Freeman

MACDONALD YOUNG BOOKS

At the edge of a dark jungle
in Africa, where the grassy
plains begin, a herd
of zebras was grazing
peacefully in the warm
evening air. One of them
was a young female
named Shanti.

Shanti was beautiful –
the most beautiful zebra
ever. Her soft brown eyes
stared dreamily at the
setting sun. Nothing could
disturb the peace and quiet.

Nothing? The zebras pricked up
their ears. They froze.

Suddenly, the mighty roar
of a lion filled the air.

The frightened zebras took to their heels.
The herd raced across the plain, their hooves
pounding. But Shanti was tired. Her stomach
hurt and now her friends were
nowhere in sight.

Hyenas howled in the distance.
Shanti trembled and looked around.
Where did everyone go?

"Shanti! Shanti!" Some monkeys poked out their heads
and disappeared again in a game of hide and seek.
"Shanti! Shanti!"
Stop that monkey business,"
Shanti said crossly,
"and tell me where
my friends are!"

The monkeys
came out one by one.
"We haven't seen them,
Shanti. Why don't you
ask Isaiah the snake?
She might be able
to help you."

"Who wants my friend, Isaiah?"
boomed a voice behind her.
Startled, Shanti turned around.
"Me," she whispered.
A rhinoceros slowly lifted
his huge head.

"Isaiah is old and wise. She sees everything."
"But where can I find her?" Shanti asked.
"Go to the watering hole. She's bound to be there."

Standing by the watering hole, Shanti called Isaiah's name. She watched in breathless silence as a glistening snake, as clear as glass, slithered up a tree.

"Don't be afraid, Shanti.
You'll never be alone again,
as long as you live."

"I don't understand," Shanti
moaned. "Please tell me
which way to go."
"I can't tell you, my dear.
You'll have to find that
out for yourself."

Disappointed, Shanti walked on until
she came to a clump of palm trees. She
leaned wearily against a slender trunk.

It was soft and warm.
Warm? Shanti whinnied in delight.

These weren't palm trees,
but the long legs of a giraffe!

"Giraffe, giraffe, please
help me!" she pleaded.
But the giraffe didn't
answer. She was
sound asleep.
Shanti had
never felt
so lonely.

After several hours, she came to a river. A turtle was sitting sleepily on a log floating in the water. Shanti was just about to ask the turtle if he'd seen her friends when the log began to move.

For a moment, Shanti stood rooted to the spot. Then she ran and ran... and almost ran straight into three huge elephants.

"Whoa Shanti. Why are you so scared?"
Panting, Shanti told them what had happened. About the lion who had attacked the zebra herd. About the mischievous monkeys, the enormous rhinoceros and the mysterious words of Isaiah the snake. She told them about the log that was really a crocodile and about her loneliness when the giraffe wouldn't wake up.

"Don't worry, Shanti. We won't leave you. We'll trumpet as loud as we can to let the zebra herd know that you're here."

"Thank you," said Shanti, feeling very relieved.
She was tired, so tired that she lay down in a
safe place near the three elephants.

The first rays of the sun shone down on her stripes.
"Isaiah was right," Shanti sighed in relief.
"I'm not alone." Lying in the tall grass,
she gave birth to a son.

Shanti bent down and started to lick her colt. Suddenly, she raised her head and sniffed – she recognised a familiar smell.

The herd appeared just as the tiny zebra was eagerly drinking his first milk. Surrounded by her friends, Shanti proudly watched her newborn son. And she named him Uzuri, which means beauty.

Bookpoint (Wayland) Aug '01
M+G